WHAT IF

WHAT IF

An *In Too Deep* Interlude

Original Publication Date: March 17th, 2022
First Paperback Edition: July 18th, 2022
ISBN: 979-8-9851404-1-5

1 3 5 7 9 10 8 6 4 2 US032422NFB

Published by Nicole Fiorina Books, Inc.

Cover design by Ashes & Vellichor

nicole *nf.* fiorina

AN *IN TOO DEEP* INTERLUDE

WHAT IF WHAT IF WHAT IF WHAT IF

NICOLE FIORINA

ALSO BY NICOLE FIORINA

Stay with Me Trilogy
Stay with Me

Even When I'm Gone

Now Open Your Eyes

Tales of Weeping Hollow
Hollow Heathens

Bone Island *(coming soon)*

Linc & Lo
Going Going Gone: a prequel

City of Angels: a rockstar romance *(coming soon)*

Ty & Kate
What If: an interlude

In Too Deep: a rap god romance *(coming soon)*

My name is Tyler Hendrix, and there used to be a beat inside my head. I'm confident I was born with it and the only one who heard it. The constant pulse was more than music. For years, I depended on it, like a born-again addict.

Until one day, a single gunshot took more than my beat away.

I've been searching for it ever since.

PLAYLIST

https://spoti.fi/3IBQQmA

HAPPIER THAN EVER - EDIT / BILLIE EILISH

ALREADY DEAD / JUICE WRLD

NO SLEEP TILL BROOKLYN / BEASTIE BOYS

MAKE IT HOT / LL COOL J

INTO YOUR ARMS (FEAT. AVA MAX) / WITT LOWRY

THIS CITY / SAM FISCHER

25 TO LIFE / EMINEM

For Michael.

Thank you for bringing me back.

THE ART
YOU CREATE IS
IMMORTAL

NEW YORK

UNITED STATES OF AMERICA

43°N 75°

11:36 AM

NEW YORK CITY HAD ONCE MADE MUSIC. BUT on this day, awful noise streamed through my helpless ears and into my head. It was a violation, a rape. At this point, I'd rather hear nothing.

Despite the noise, the air was fresh, and SoHo was alive.

Gemma pulled me out of my daze, and I was right back to where I'd been all along: sitting in front of her, trapped in a relationship, with the sultry sun crawling higher between a crack in the cast-iron buildings. Its rays against my face.

Gemma lounged in the shade under a black and white striped umbrella, oversized black sunglasses hiding the top half of her face. Car horns and the soft music playing from the outdoor speakers muffled her words—or muddled my ears. I couldn't be sure. I was hungover, brain damaged, still in sweats, and hadn't slept in over twenty-four hours.

I popped another pill into my mouth to keep myself from standing, from pacing. To keep my thoughts from racing. I tried focusing on Gemma's lips to make out the words she was saying.

All I could see was the gash of nude lipstick spearing across her bleached teeth, but I couldn't tell her this. I could hardly get a word out. I blinked, wishing her away.

Gemma's voice raised an octave from across the bistro table when she said, "And Kendall, of all people." A manicured claw came down on the table, shaking her pomegranate mimosa. "It took me a week to get out of bed after what that *pute* called me. Do you remember?" An ugly Chinese Crested pup lapping Voss from a marble bowl next to Gemma skittered away, a scrawny bent tail wagging from between its owner's legs beside us. "How could you do this to me?"

"I—"

"No, Ty. I don't want to hear it."

Just don't give a fuck trapped in my brain. Repeating. There was no point. I didn't have an excuse for what happened between Kendall and me. I had been drunk and out of my mind, one thing leading to another. It was how the story always went. My *fuck this* mindset evolved as the world turned. And the world would always turn.

Between the long intervals of surrendering to chemical demons and blacking out, the music industry had been screaming in my ear. They wanted me locked in a room with a mic to produce music that sounded like the next, lyrics that didn't stand out from the rest, my pen's damage folded and tucked in my pocket to never see the light of day. I'd heard the shit going viral. If what I produced didn't sound like what was buzzing, it would be trash to them, anyway.

I'd flipped the switch on rap just before I missed the days when everyone wasn't tone-deaf. A time when being different meant something. Hip Hop was fucked, so I gave it the middle finger.

Producers wanted a carbon copy. Not an original.

The real Ty Hendrix could no longer exist here.

I was okay with that because if I did, so did everything else.

For three months, Gemma was my only constant. I needed challenge and passion in all aspects of my awoken life, so I spent most of our *relationship* getting a rise out of her, pissing her off to see if she cared about me at all or only the contract. Three more months and our contract would end. I could escape this shit-show of a *showmance,* but my guilty conscience would never escape me.

I swung my head to the side.

I tuned her out and peered down Lower Manhattan.

Gemma carried on.

The neighborhood was a picturesque backdrop for high-end crowds with boutiques, art galleries, and elegant restaurants—a living, breathing urban vein in the heart of New York.

Girls grouped together on street corners, phones out and snapping pictures of us from behind designer shopping bags as big as their daddy's credit card limits.

Gemma snapped her finger in front of my face with a groan, stealing my attention from on-lookers. "Are you seriously checking girls out?" A sigh. "You just can't help yourself, can you?"

"Gemma, give me a break." It was the first time I could get anything out between bits and pieces she fired at me. I'd only caught keywords and dodged the rest.

The pup looked at me from between its owner's legs. Its tongue hung like a limp pink dick from the side of its mouth. Thirteen wiry hairs stood straight on a balding head, almost like it was embarrassed to be here, too.

"You want to go back to L.A., is that what this is?"

"Fuck, that would be amazing, but we both know that can't happen. The only thing I need right now is for you to get off my back and a pillow to shove my face into." I sat back in the chair and stretched my long legs out under the table. "This screams attention." I waved my hand toward the on-lookers. "But this is what you wanted, isn't it? It's very Gemma of you. A fight on public display. Make me out to be the bad guy in this."

A tear slipped from under her glasses.

I rolled my head back. "Oh, here come the waterworks."

"I don't want to fight with you," she mumbled through a sniffle, patting her bronzed cheekbone with a cloth napkin. "I just don't want my boyfriend fucking my enemy."

"Should I have taken home your other fake friend instead?"

"Who? Lyla? I could have been okay with that."

As much as that thought didn't surprise me, and something I should have expected her to say, I was still stunned to hear her admit it out loud. I slumped in the chair with no fight in me. Just dust. "You're a real piece of work."

"You just don't understand ..." her voice trailed when the paparazzi popped up from behind a Tesla. If there was a time and place I wanted the paps to come and rescue me from a situation, it was now. But they didn't. All the expensive cameras kept their distance so Gemma could yell at me in peace.

They shot over a hundred stills within the last twenty-five seconds. I imagined what they were thinking: *rapper, Ty Hendrix, was making his darling model-actress girlfriend cry.* The ratings for her debut movie would sky-rocket, and I'd get flooded with more hate mail. Direct messages. It didn't take much effort to *select all, delete.*

If people wanted to say insane things about me, form opinions, that was their right. None of it could touch me anymore.

"Girls are vindictive. The only reason Kendall even had sex with you was to get to me," Gemma said, her voice background noise.

The corner of my head throbbed. A scar sliced through my right brow, and I pressed my thumb into it to make the ache go away. The scar was from when my brother, Linc, split the skin with his knuckles. A constant reminder of how much he hated me.

I shoved a hand into my pocket and pulled out a pack of cigarettes.

"Do you have to do that here? It's so rude," Gemma barked.

I glanced up, my hair falling into my eyes. A bright light bounced off my glasses and blinded me. Without them, I couldn't see, but I still pulled them off, raked my fingers through my hair, and looked back to see where it had come from.

Across the cobblestone street, a waitress balanced a tray of dirty dishes and wiped down a table. She was as clear as a daydream, with her blonde hair pulled back in a ponytail and white strands framing her face. A crisp white apron hugged her waist below a sea-colored blouse. A single *thump*, like a pulse, vibrated in my head.

California, I thought. The waitress reminded me of California.

A city bike zoomed down the street, and paparazzi jumped out of the way, knocking the waitress against the side of the building. The tray piled with dishes crashed to the floor. The sun blared. *Click, click, click.*

"Tyler!" Gemma growled. My phone buzzed in my pocket. Chaos everywhere. I stood and pushed the chair out from under me. "Tyler, what are you doing?"

Then I was walking, chasing the beat, the cobblestone street beneath my Nikes and Gemma's voice behind me. The rhythmic thumping grew louder and with each step. My sights were set on the waitress, and I didn't stop until the paparazzi surrounded me and she was in front of me. Their *click, click, clicks* were like cotton swabs in my ears.

The waitress had her back to me, about to bend down to pick up the broken glass. She flipped her ponytail to one side, and the blonde ends rolled off her shoulder and grazed her collarbone. *Thump, thump, thump*, like a bass in my ears. The morning air carried the sound and everything she did.

There it was, in my head, my low and steady beat.

I was right where I was supposed to be.

Glass crunched under my feet. I reached for her arm to spin her around before she had a chance to bend down. Large blue eyes looked up at me, bouncing with confusion.

I touched her face lightly with the tips of my fingers.

And then I kissed her.

11:49 AM

THE MOMENT OUR LIPS TOUCHED, THE WAITRESS PULLED away and slapped me.

My head twisted to the side, a sting burning my cheek.

I licked my lips, tasting cherry Chapstick on my tongue, and smiled. I'd deserved that. It had seemed vain to start with, 'Hi, my name is Tyler Hendrix, and I still don't give a fuck, but I missed that sound.'

Click, click, click.

"Ty Hendrix, who is this woman to you?" came from my left. "Is this why you and Gemma Perez were arguing? Have you been cheating on her this whole time?" came from my right. And I couldn't force away my grin.

When I looked back at the waitress, I noticed the freckle beside her right eye beneath her brow, the only sweet feature on her angry face.

I'd witnessed a bucket full of emotions in girls' eyes before. Infatuation, nervousness, lust. But never a rocket ship about to take off. Her eyes were narrowed at me, pounding out anger between blinks. Irises hot and intense.

I took a step back, my fingers still wrapped around her arm. I let her go.

A crowd pushed us from all sides, when a hand came between us—twenty-four karats wrapped around the wrist—and flung orange juice at the waitress, soaking her.

The waitress stood frozen with her arms stiff at her sides, angry eyes gone and squeezed shut. The cute little freckle beside her eye had folded in half.

When she opened her eyes again, both of us just stood there. Our shocked gazes stuck together as OJ slid down her face, dripping from her ponytail and jawline. Pulp clung to her lashes, her blonde strands. The blue blouse was drenched and transparent, sticking to the waitress's skin and showing off a black lace bra.

Her nostrils flared, and her pupils grew ten sizes.

I caught the name *Kate* printed on her nametag pinned to her breast pocket just before she ducked between the crowd. The thumping slowed, quieted.

"Kate," I said, but it wasn't loud enough. "Kate, wait!"

I went to grab her hand to bring the beat back, but she slipped through my fingers. The crowd cornered me, boxed me out.

I peered over heads, and Kate disappeared into the restaurant.

Cameras crowded me, questions hitting me from every which way. I clasped my fingers together and settled my folded hands on my head, spinning around for an opening.

Across the street, Gemma was gone, and the Chinese Crested pup was brave enough to return to its water bowl.

Kissing her was a bold move, a quest to make the noise stop—to shut everyone up and be with the beat again. The same beat I hadn't heard in over six years. In a way, the dumb kiss did all these things, but for only a moment.

My actions came off as petty, but everyone had a breaking point. I didn't care about the consequences. I didn't care about the story they would spin. But for some reason, I cared about the turmoil it caused the waitress.

I pushed people out of the way, trying to get to the door Kate had disappeared behind. I reached for the door handle, and the world went silent once I was inside, like someone placed noise-canceling headphones over my ears and transported me somewhere else.

An erotic and masculine scent drifted under my nose, and a collision of string music penetrated the silence. A slow rise of violins, cellos, harps, and guitars. If it were at all possible, in a whispered rush, the sad music managed to make it feel like my heart was aching.

I dropped my forehead to the closed restaurant door, breathed in, and breathed out. The crowd shoved and pushed and pressed their faces against the glass to peer inside from the other side. I pulled away when a man with greased back hair tapped the door with his finger. "What's going on, Ty? You can't hide in there all day."

"This is private property," I said, flipping the *open* sign over between us and twisting the lock with a *click*. "Go stalk someone else and make them famous."

When I turned, a woman appeared in front of me. She was short but still in my face. Wrinkles crested the corners of her brown eyes, around her mouth. Red bangs covered her forehead, and the rest of her hair was held back by a giant claw clip.

A combat gaze zoned in on me. "You can't be in here."

"I just want to talk to her," I said, holding my palms up in surrender and seeing Kate behind the counter picking pulp from her hair. Her posture was harsh, and her fingers shook each time they stripped a strand. My phone was continuously going off inside my pocket, and my brain spun, but I ignored it all, trying to pull myself together.

I took a side-step. This time, my words were for Kate—"Please, let me fix this."

"Fix." Kate *hmphed*, shook her head back and forth. "Ty Hendrix wants to fix this."

She said my name as if I wasn't in the room. Was her caustic tone because of the tabloids? The social media rants? I'd been too busy wasting away. I hadn't sobered up long enough to see the picture the public painted of me. It didn't matter because she was right. I didn't fix things, I ruined them.

My gaze flitted over the restaurant in one quick sweep to take in my surroundings and think about what I would say. A long emerald velvet bench stretched along a white brick wall on one side. I only thought of emerald because it was the same color as my little sister's eyes. She had these emerald glass eyes that haunted me long after she died.

Wooden chairs slid under bistro-style tables with hammered gold edges. Nude paintings covered the white brick walls. A French twist under the soft glow. Paintings of naked breasts, couples kissing with tongue, and intercourse splashed the brick wall like it were no big deal. Like I was the one out of place in this tiny gem of a space.

I dragged in a breath and settled my eyes back on Kate. "I'm probably everything they say I am, but I can at least try to make this right."

"*He can try to make this right,*" Kate mocked under her breath, soaking the ends of her hair in a stainless-steel sink.

"Why are you talking as if I'm not standing right here?"

"She does that," the woman said beside me, and I'd forgotten she was there. "It's a way to distance herself from the situation."

Kate turned off the water and dropped her palms on top of the counter, my attention snapping back to her.

"Trish! Don't talk to him," Kate seethed, wet hair sticking to the side of her cheek. "Maybe if we ignore him, he'll just go away."

"I'm not going away."

Trish turned her eyes back to Kate and shrugged. "He's not going away."

What's happening? I stepped toward Kate. "Just hear me out. I can replace your clothes and those ..." I peered over the counter and scrunched my face, "hideous shoes, I don't even know what to call them."

Kate narrowed her eyes. She was very good at it. "They're leather."

"They're ugly."

"They're Stuart Weitzman."

"I don't even know who that is."

"Your girlfriend is a model."

"Yeah, that doesn't help my case in the least."

Kate groaned. "This is stupid. Why am I even talking to you?"

"Because I'm charming. I can show you if you'd let me."

"And he's cocky, ladies and gentlemen," she said, shutting off the water and raising her hands in the air.

"Please stop doing that."

"When you're not partying or causing a scene, you still manage to create problems for others when everything's going perfectly fine. Tell me, Ty. When's the last time you had your fix?" she asked, and a memory of taking a pill with my mimosa whipped by. I felt my face fall. Literally, felt it fall with her accuracy. Kate tilted her head and squinted her eyes. "God, are you fucked up *right now*?"

To make myself seem more stable, I laid a hand over the counter and felt paper slide beneath it. It was a letter. *Three months' notice* was written in bold red letters across the top of the page.

I picked it up to examine it further when Kate reached over the bar between us and snatched it out of my hand. "You shouldn't pry into other people's personal business."

"That's hypocritical, considering you all drink up my personal business for entertainment."

"Hey, you asked for that life."

"No, I didn't. And you didn't tell me that you owned this restaurant." Restaurant owners didn't wear aprons and bus tables at their own establishments. Or maybe they did, but not in neighborhoods like this. Cities like this. They were too busy having drinks and networking and showing off their bank accounts to clients.

"It's not something I go around advertising."

She was humble without making a show of it. I liked that about her. It was one of the few things between her cutting replies and narrowed eyes. "Don't get me wrong, I don't see what's so special about Gotham city, but having something that's all yours in one of the most famous cities in the world? I'm impressed."

Kate swept a strand from her eyes with the back of her hand and looked down at the letter, sadness creeping along her features. "Not for long." Her grief faded fast, and anger took her over again. It all unfolded in front of me, the spiral of emotions. She crumpled the paper into a ball and chucked it across the restaurant. It landed into the trashcan without touching the rim, and I felt it in my chest as if it scraped the rim of my ribcage.

This SoHo daydream loved the restaurant. Almost as much as I once loved music. I didn't know which was worse: knowing you were about to lose the only thing that mattered, or it being taken away from you without warning. I didn't know, but I wanted to help. I didn't have the best reputation, but I had the means. Money. A name. All the things that I would have once died for.

"Let me help. With your restaurant."

"What makes you think I want anything from you?"

"You don't, I know that. But your ego doesn't pay your bills, and I can help. But I'll need something in return."

She leaned on her hip. "Of course, you do."

I was stuck in New York for another three months. If I wanted to survive this contract with Gemma, this seemed like the only way to ignite something in this city after what it had done to me. After all, Kate was the reason the beat had returned.

She *was* the beat, and I wanted to stay with her a while longer.

"Spend twelve hours with me. I'll pay you to show me around. To introduce me to all the things that make this city so great. Change my mind. Make me fall in love with it."

It was the first time Kate smiled. And when Kate smiled, the soft beat inside my head *thumped, thumped, thumped.* "Love is a crazy woman, Ty. A crazy woman that has claws to scratch you whenever she wants," she said. "Do you really want New York City tearing apart your west coast heart?"

I was sick and tired of the *bad-meets-evil* mindset. It was about the city as much as it was about the music.

It had been too long since music made me feel good. Tough. Powerful. Lyrics had been my confidence to throw the first punch, convey a message, or just bleed out. Once upon a time, rap had been my liquor of choice and the only pill I'd swallow.

A part of me, the part that was sober and awake and starving, was still famished for it all. Stomach hurting. Delirious. Weak.

"Yes. Yes, I do. And I'll even throw in a sweetener: no alcohol, drugs, or sex for twelve hours."

DA-DA
DUM

3:13 PM

WE WERE ABOUT TO MEET ON THE SIDEWALK.

It always began for us on the sidewalk.

I'd given her a couple of hours to shower and change her clothes, so my late morning had been spent trying to sober up with sleep to prepare for our twelve hours together, but I couldn't sit still, and the clock raced with my anticipation of seeing her again.

I leaned against the glass storefront of Now or Never Coffee Shop—the place we agreed to meet—downing an orange ginger latte that was promised to cure my hangover by the barista behind the counter.

It was early afternoon, and the sun was sick and high above me, throwing up its rays all over the city. If she didn't show up, it was only a short walk around the corner to the SoHo Grand Hotel, and she could forget this had happened. We would never see each other again, and my manager would spin a story to buy his shady client time until some other elite loser of society did something stupid.

The public would move on. They always did.

I hid under a snapback and behind shades—my eyeglasses left at the hotel—scrolling through my phone in one hand, my empty latte cup in the other. That's when I looked up.

I noticed her from two blocks away.

When Kate walked past people, they turned their heads, her long tanned legs like two sticks poking out of a leopard-print mini skirt. She wore hideous black cowboy boots, and her hair swayed under a newsboy hat. I adjusted my shades, spotting blood-red lipstick splashed across her pouty lips as she walked toward me. Reminders of the slight taste of her sparked my tongue.

I didn't realize how long I'd been staring until I looked down and noticed my phone screen went black. I shoved it into my pocket when she neared, and I pushed my back off the glass wall.

"You showed up," I said, suddenly feeling foolish around her. Before, she was beautiful, even with orange juice dripping down her face. Although now, as she stood before me, she was a sexy kind of beautiful. Bold and loud.

"Keys, phone," she said, stopping in front of me, lifting her head to meet my eyes. She had her palm out between us. "Gimme."

I laughed. "I'm not giving you my phone."

"Places are much like people," she began, digging into my pockets, and I let her. I was amused by her audacity and her hand so close to my ... "You can only see a new place objectively once. At first glance. After that, your opinion of a place will be tainted. You already hate it. It's already tainted for whatever reason, and if our deal is for me to make you fall in love with it, we need your undivided attention. Hence, I'll need your phone." She held up my phone between us, clasped between nude painted fingernails.

I liked how she referred to the city and her as we. "I respect your commitment. Do you give *everything* you do one hundred percent?"

Kate smiled, and I could tell we would have fun together. "Like I said, Ty, places are like people. There's a reason we have skulls around our brains and cages around our hearts. Everyone wants to be loved, but no one wants to get hurt. And you will fall in love again, but only after this place breaks your heart. What's an epic love story, if not a little suffering?"

"A tragedy."

Kate's face fell.

The first time I'd come here was six years ago. It was for my first show at Madison Square Garden.

I'd only stayed for a mere twelve hours, a return plane ticket to home in my pocket as soon as I stepped onto New York pavement. At the time, it was easy to tuck away California when it begged to be compared to a city that begged to be loved. It had been easy to be blinded by the city lights, ambition and drive so full it spilled out of me. I hadn't settled in. I hadn't met city dwellers. I hadn't tasted their food.

I'd put on a fucking show, later earning me both a Grammy for songwriting and Best New Artist at the Teen Choice Awards in my debut year, which lit the media on fire. I'd shown up to neither award shows, not giving a damn about the trophies.

But Kate was right about one thing: the great NYC had become tainted in those twelve short hours I'd spent here the first time. And what she didn't know was, this place had already broken my fucking heart.

A contract and overwhelming guilt forced me here a second time. "Sometimes you have to do things you don't want to do. You have to do what's expected of you," my manager, Colorado, had said. "Pay your dues." So, I signed the contract, met the people, tasted the food. All love lost, no love found.

Kate tucked the phone away into a zipped pocket in her purse, a torn paper from one of my spiral notebooks sticking to it. "What's this?" she said, unfolding the page to read the scribble.

I snatched it from her fingers. "I'll take that."

"You are writing," she stated. "Afraid I won't like it?"

"It's gibberish. Everyone's raps look terrible on paper."

Her gaze lingered on me, searching, then she turned and walked away. I paused for a moment to tuck the words back into my pocket. My eyes fell onto her cute little ass in that skirt. A shit-eating grin consumed my face, and I took off into a jog after her.

"Now that you disconnected me from the world, where are we off to first?" I asked, my hands feeling empty at my sides. "The Statue of Liberty? The Empire State Building?" I turned, walking backward to face her. "You're going to make me wear one of those 'I Love New York' shirts, aren't you? Because that's where I draw the line."

"First of all"—Kate grabbed my shoulders and spun me around, her eyes dancing to my antics— "don't walk backward here, it's not cool, and you could cause an accident."

"And second of all?"

"Just don't think about it, okay?"

I glanced down at her, seeing her try to hide a smile inside those red-painted lips. "Okay."

3:21 PM

I F MANHATTAN WERE THE HEART OF NEW YORK, THE subway stations were the lungs. It breathed us in, breathed us out.

People were in full swing, bustling up and down the stairs. Some with music blaring from headphones, others in groups and trying to stay together without bumping shoulders with strangers.

Once we reached the underground platform, a bad breath of weed and sweat and urine blew in my face. Paint peeled off the walls and ceiling like scabs, leaving behind dirt and grime. Litter piled in the corners, empty cups and torn brown paper bags high like something I'd see in Linc's studio apartment back in Santa Monica. We walked by words that had been graffitied on the wall: *the art you create is immortal.*

Kate's fingers wrapped around my bicep as she walked close beside me, a debate brewing between us.

"Who the fuck was cooler than Run-DMC?" I asked, and Kate threw her head back with a laugh, then shook her head. "Exactly. No one."

She rolled her eyes. "Beastie Boys."

"Okay, okay. Both are in my top three. Still not cooler, though."

She turned her body toward me just enough to shut the rest of the world out and whispered, "Three rules, and you'll be a subway pro: pay no attention to what everyone else is doing. If you fall, get right back up. Ride with honesty." She paused. "Oh, and don't touch anything."

"That's four." I looked around. "Do you ride the subway every day? Alone?"

"This is why I have rules."

Bells rang around us.

Prompts from a loudspeaker echoed above us.

The whirr inside the station pulled me in every direction until a subway car lurched forward before coming to a halt. Doors slid open with a whoosh of stale air. I took off my shades and settled them on my hat, then dropped my hand to the back of my neck and squeezed.

Kate's hand landed on my back, urging me to enter the subway.

We stepped on. The bell came again. The doors slid closed.

All the plastic seats were taken, forcing Kate and me to stand.

When the subway car lurched forward again, I staggered with it, my body colliding with Kate's. I reached for something to hold, and Kate stopped me with a shake of the head and a light touch of her hand against my wrist.

"Don't touch anything," she said. Her hand drifted down my side, and she patted my thigh. "Part your legs and find balance." The subtle touch sent a shiver down my marrow, a heartbeat in my ears. She managed to crack me open and force me to take a deep breath to mask it. We were so close I tried to avoid looking her in the eyes so she wouldn't see what it did to me.

A homeless man splayed out on the bench spoke nonsense beside us. His beard was matted, scum in the creases of his wrinkles. He looked as if he hadn't showered in over a month. The stench of booze and roadkill permeated off him.

There was a military patch on his cap, and I assumed he was one of the many war Veterans the system had dumped after serving our country. It was a sad sight to see though common in California, too.

It hadn't hit me until this moment. It didn't matter what city, state, or part of the world we were in. It didn't matter what we did for others or the sacrifices we'd made. No one was immune to people turning their backs on us.

It made me think of my fans. How far was I willing to go before they turned their back on me, too?

"Hey, girl. Come sit on my face," the homeless Veteran said, his arm reaching for Kate's thigh.

I blocked his hand. "Show some respect, man."

He laughed. "You going to show her some respect?"

Kate stood solid with an impenetrable force surrounding her, ignoring him as if this was something she dealt with day in and day out.

A woman standing behind Kate grimaced. A laugh cracked from a man to my right. We were all squeezed into a small place with nowhere to run. I laid my hands on Kate's shoulders, turning us so that my back was facing the homeless man, and she was out of reach. Guilt slammed into me for doing it. For turning my back on him like the rest, but I couldn't let him touch her, either. She was mine for the next twelve hours. The only face she had the option of sitting on was mine.

"Aw, c'mon, help a brother out," the drunken homeless man said.

I ignored it all and focused on Kate. Looked her in the eyes. Her breasts were pressed against my chest, and I felt every intake of breath she took.

Kate looked at me, too, her ocean blue gaze jumping about my face, perhaps noticing the heavy bead of sweat sitting on my brow from wanting to throw my fist into the homeless man's face or from weaning off the pills. It could go either way at this point.

Then Kate tore her gaze away and pulled earbuds from the hidden pocket of her mini skirt. She handed me one, its wire dangling between us.

I put the bud into my ear, and she plugged the end into her phone and played a song: *No Sleep Till Brooklyn* by the Beastie Boys.

I smiled.

DA
DUM

3:39 PM

THE SUDDEN CRAVING I HAD FOR KATE WAS TANGIBLE. And when we returned to higher ground, my fingers brushed her thigh as we stepped into the center of Time Square. A touch so simple that still managed to make something inside me come alive. It should have been the city, I thought, as the colors and lights and animated billboards jumped out and assaulted me. The square had a quality of demanding your silence and drawing all attention, making it impossible to focus on any one detail.

"Was that your first time in a subway?" she asked as we walked side by side along the sidewalk. "You looked like you wanted to throw up."

"It was an experience I'll never get used to," I said, sliding my shades back on and lowering my hat. I didn't know which way she would take that, and I didn't know how I meant it. If I were talking about Kate or the subway. If I were talking about the drunken homeless man slapping me with a dose of reality or the ache to touch her.

My thoughts were split between chaos and hunger.

Our reflections bounced off glass storefronts, the tattoos crawling up and down my right arm warping and blurring like a funhouse mirror. I looked deeply at myself, and for a moment, it seemed like I didn't have a scar on my brow at all.

A display of shoes caught my eye, and I reeled back. "Let's go in and see if they have your shoes."

Kate stopped and turned around, throwing a hand over her eyes. "No."

No? "Why not?"

"You can't just buy me the shoes."

"Uhh ...Yes, I can."

"No, I mean, they can't just be replaced." She huffed and dropped her arm to her side, hustling New Yorkers breezing past her on both sides. "Forget it, please. Let's keep going. We only have eleven and a half hours."

I took a step toward her. "Why? We can find a department store or something if this isn't the place. Don't make it a bigger deal than it is because it's no big deal for me. I want to do this."

"That's my point," she said, turning away to start walking again.

I caught her arm to stop her, turning her back around to face me. "Stop. Just for a second. I'm offering to replace your boots that got ruined, and you just went from a hundred to zero degrees so quick my head is spinning. What is it about those fucking shoes?"

"I'll tell you about the shoes when you tell me why you hate New York so much." She stood stubbornly with a peaked brow, the Gatsby hat shading half her face. I opened my mouth, my heart pounding in my chest, in my ears, but nothing came out. I'd been put on the spot before, many times, but she had a way of making me feel like I was slashed open and exposed. "Yeah, I thought so," she said with my silence.

I hated confrontation and was determined to turn this mood around, so I grazed my knuckles along her side to test her, to shatter her ice. "You know, you're sexy when you get all worked up."

She wiggled away from me, trying not to smile. It was adorable.

"We're only a few more blocks away," she said.

"Away from what?"

"My Sunday afternoon hideout."

Few more blocks, my ass. Sweat slid down my spine when we entered the used record store, and I drank in the cool air. The shop was much like a record store I would frequent back home. The old nostalgic cardboard scent of vintage vinyl reminded me of my childhood, growing up with Linc and my sister, Tanya. Each time I'd walk to the record store, it was never because I was on the hunt for a specific record. Linc and Dad were the ones into vinyl, and I'd always spent the little cash I made from rap battles on cassettes.

"Follow me," she whispered, and her voice sounded like a beat I'd never heard of. One I wanted to produce.

Kate exchanged quick hellos with an old man wearing a bucket hat behind the counter, then she took off to the back and around the corner. I followed her. "LL Cool J is one of my favorites," I heard her say as I turned the corner. L was in my top ten, and suddenly, I wanted her tongue down my throat. Wrapped around my dick. Anywhere. Desperately. With *Doin' It* playing in the background.

I swallowed. "Really?" We were in a back room dedicated to the man. His posters, records, cassettes, and CDs were everywhere in the closet space.

"On vinyl. It has this crackling sound and ..." she hummed like she was tasting the beat on her lips. She stood on the toes of her cowboy boots, reaching up to grab an old record player from the dusty top shelf.

I would have helped her but couldn't. I was too busy staring at the crescents of her ass cheeks peeking from under her skirt.

"It's okay we're back here. The owner used to vibe with L," she said. "L's from Bay Shore but back in the day, he would stop in all the time and drop a lot of money in here to keep this place alive. At least that's what Greg, the owner, always tells me. Now Greg's pushing sixty and still rockin' those wacky neon balloon pants because *hip hop isn't something you do but something you are. A way of life.*" She landed back on her feet and faced the wall to plug the record player in. "Hey, you know what I was thinking?" she asked suddenly, facing me again while the intro of *Make It Hot* sizzled on the player.

I snapped my eyes up and straightened my posture. "What? What were you thinking?"

"What does your girlfriend think about what you did and this arrangement we have?"

"It's not exactly what it seems like between us, and I couldn't give a fuck about what Gemma thinks."

Kate cocked her head. "Does *she* know this?"

"Yes."

"And what if I was married?"

"Are you?"

"I could be. What if I was married, and you just kissed me like you did. You really should think before you act, Ty. It could have been anyone with a husband and kids or psychotic boyfriend, and now it's all over the internet." Kate's eyes widened with entire oceans inside them. "And what if said *crazy boyfriend* finds out and is abusive and strangles her to death? You don't take anyone else's life into account. You're impulsive and can be downright disrespectful in the most ridiculous, passive way. It's great for music but horrible for forming any type of relationship."

"Are you fucking with me right now?"

"Serious as a heart attack."

A smirk played on my lips. "I wonder what this psychotic boyfriend would think if I kissed you twice."

"You should at least ask him first."

I patted my pockets, forgetting she had my cell. I put my thumb and finger to my ear, mimicking a phone. "Hey, I'm looking for Psychotic Boyfriend of Kate ..." my words faded, and I placed a hand over my pinky and whispered, "What's your last name?"

"You're an idiot."

I returned to my imaginary call. "Yeah, man, I'm here. Look, I kissed your girl, hope you don't mind." Kate's face turned red. "I plan on doing it again, doing it right this time if you know what I mean. Make her all hot and bothered. That is, if she'll let me. She did say I needed to talk to you first. I'm trying to work on taking other people's lives into account"—I paused, displaying shock and holding my palm against my chest. "No shit, bro." I covered the fake phone again with my hand and whispered to Kate. "Psychotic Imaginary Boyfriend said he doesn't want you anymore and to go to hell."

Kate lunged at me, laughing and ready to attack. *Make It Hot* turned on the table behind her, crackling in the small space.

I gripped her forearms, keeping her close until her laughter faded. The mood in the room changed, charged. It turned thick and heavy, the aftertaste of her still tingling on my lips. I chanced a look around the room. We were all alone.

"Kiss me," I said.

"Kiss you?"

"I'm asking you this time. I'm a changed man, Kate."

"I don't know. My imaginary boyfriend just dumped me. Don't you think it's too soon—"

I dipped my head down and crushed my mouth to hers, the force taking her against the shelved wall. The kiss followed her. Pinned her there.

I parted my mouth, and her tongue thrust inside, every nerve ending meeting liquid until I was hard and stretched against my sweats. I felt like I could die if we stopped. *Fuck*, I could die kissing her forever. I could kiss her, die, reincarnate, live, repeat. Kate moaned when I took her bottom lip into my mouth, pulling back only to slip my tongue inside her mouth again, tasting her. She was a blend of sweet addiction.

And the song on the record player changed with us.

DA

DA

4:42 PM

KATE HAD WALKED OUT OF THE RECORD STORE with a hand over her mouth, cheeks hot and flushed. I'd turned my hat back around and shadowed my face, wishing I could access her thoughts. If she were replaying what had happened back at the record store like I was. If she wanted more like I did. It was only a kiss, but it was enough to keep the picture of her naked pinned in my mind, hung on the walls of my skull.

We hadn't said a word to each other since we left the record store, but she did rap an Eminem song under her breath. I wondered if it were something she did when she was nervous. The way she knew every word kept the beat with me and steady inside my head. Even when we'd stopped to grab pizza from a hole-in-the-wall joint, it seemed Kate used small talk with the marinara-splashed Yankee behind the pizza bar to distract herself from me. She didn't want to eat, though, and told Frankie she was too worked up and to cut me a *mad good* slice. Whatever that meant.

In no hurry, we walked side by side as city slickers blew past us, phones glued to their ears and New York accents flooding mine. Kate tied her hair back and off her shoulders. Tiny beads of sweat like diamonds glistened along the nape of her neck. Her rosy cheeks hadn't faded, and her red lipstick was smudged. All the subtleties from our one-on-one that had made her come undone.

With a humorous smile, I took a bite of the wonky and fat slice of heaven, fresh mozzarella and pepperoni sliding off and dripping onto the paper plate I held beneath it. It was crazy to think that for a moment, and for as long as I'd been making music, she was the one who'd made me feel gifted.

"Okay, stop," Kate said, grabbing my arm and breaking the silence. "You can't eat it like that. You have to fold it in half." I froze, my mouth full. "Just give it to me, let me show you." She took the pizza from my hand, bent the crust in half, turned her head, and took a cosmic bite. Mozzarella stretched from the corners of her mouth as she pulled it away. "Oh, this is good," she said, turning away from me, ready to take another bite.

I leaned forward, reaching for my slice. "Whoa, nuh-uh. If you wanted pizza, you should have ordered your own slice," I said through my mouthful, taking it back. I swallowed, watching cheese strings dangle from her bottom lip. "And I'll take this, too." I picked the mozzarella from the corner of her mouth and dropped it into mine.

Kate's face squished. "You're disgusting."

"Awe, don't act like I haven't been inside that mouth of yours."

She slapped my shoulder, and a laugh cracked out of me.

It was easy, falling back into step on the sidewalk with her.

Dirtbags passing us looked at her twice. Women, too. She never noticed, but I did every time. Walking next to her made me feel like both a god and a mortal. For once, no one was looking at me. They were all looking at her. It allowed me to breathe, a sense of being free.

I trashed the paper plate and swung an arm around her shoulder, dropping my mouth to Kate's ear. "We have ten more hours together. Once three AM strikes, the sweetener of no alcohol and sex is off the table."

I'd never planned to fuck this waitress I kissed back in SoHo, and I couldn't tell if she wanted me, too, but I'd be a liar if I thought she wasn't the reason my beat was rising from the silence.

It was only a fifteen-minute walk to Central Park. The sun hung in the sky like it was about to faceplant at any moment. Lamp posts glowed, and trees created a tunnel around a thick concrete walkway. Scattered light flickered through tree branches like strobe lights as we strolled between green benches lining each side of the pathway.

Kate took a seat, and I sat beside her, stretching out my legs. It was the first chance I had to sit down in hours.

Beside me, Kate lowered her cap. "You see that lady reading the book to your left?"

I hadn't noticed until I turned my head.

Sitting about twenty-five feet away, an old woman was sitting on the same green bench on the opposite side with a paperback opened and resting on her lap. She sat alone, silver hair curling around her hat and rags hanging off her bones. Despite looking breakable, the world she was lost in was unshakeable.

Kate sighed at my side. Like she let go of all the burdens in the world in that one breath. "In too deep."

I looked at Kate from the corner of my eyes. "What's that?"

"That's what the book is called. *In Too Deep.*"

"Never heard of it."

"She wrote it," Kate said, her eyes pointing at the old woman. "Her name is Gertie Ellis. She sits there on the same bench at the same time every day and reads that same book."

My gaze bounced back to old Gertie. The label would have to put a gun to my temple to force me to perform the music they made me record. The thought of listening to it on repeat felt like rape. The reason I refused to let it go to the public. "Why?"

"Reliving. It's the only thing Gertie has left."

"You read the book, didn't you?"

Kate nodded. "She marked it as fiction. People can't judge you when it's marked as fiction. To everyone else, it's make-believe, but to her, it's a lucid dream. After all this time, she can't escape from her past mistakes. It's like she reads the book over and over as if something would change. Like the answers are right there in front of her, and she can't figure out where it all went wrong. It breaks my heart."

I couldn't look away from the woman. "How do you know all this?"

"The girl in the story is named Evie," Kate said instead, and how she knew all this wasn't as important as the story she was about to tell me.

So, I listened.

I watched the woman from twenty-five feet away with Kate's voice in my ear.

"Evie lived in New York but spent her summers in Florida because that's where her aunt lived, and one scorching Florida summer, she met a boy and fell in love. His name was Peter, and it was that young, first love. The kind that never really goes away, you know? And summer after summer, year after year, she'd go back to Florida and see him. They had this connection that it didn't matter what stage they were at in their life or who they were with at the time. When they were together, everything else disappeared.

"After about three years of this, the distance got hard. Peter loved Florida, and Evie loved New York. Both were too stubborn to leave, and eventually, Evie met a man in the city. I forgot his name, so let's just call him Matt."

"Matt. Nice."

"Matt and Evie were on fire. Their relationship was passionate. Like fiery, hot, angry, possessive ..."

I laughed. "Okay, okay. I get the point."

"But each year, Evie still went to Florida to see Peter. She could never let him go, and Peter knew about Matt but didn't care. Peter even had a girlfriend of his own, but it was like a pact. This connection they had was too strong to care when they were together, even though neither one of them would sacrifice leaving their home.

"Back in New York, the passion eventually turned toxic with Matt, and the moment Evie realized this, was about to pack her bags for Florida, she found out she was pregnant with Matt's baby. In her mind, for her child, she had to make it work with Matt. See if having this baby would make a change between them." Kate's tone dropped in degree, and I looked at her. She'd taken her eyes off the woman, and her stare hit the ground. "It didn't. After they married and the baby was born, the toxicity turned to abuse. The emotional kind."

The chill of her statement ran cold in my veins. It wasn't about what she'd said but how she'd said, and the way her voice dropped stuck in the summer air.

"Evie was between a rock and a hard place. She couldn't take her kid out of New York, and the only thing left to do was stay and give up a life with the only man she ever loved to raise her child, thinking she was making the best decision for her little girl. Because it would be wrong taking a child away from their father. Plus, Matt had rights too. The state didn't believe in the bruises they couldn't see.

"So, Evie's daughter grew up watching her mom fall in and out of depression, ultimately losing a sense of herself and identity. And when the daughter turned eighteen, she couldn't stand to watch her mom waste away because she never stood up for herself. So, the daughter left New York with a vow to never end up like her mom. When the daughter had a kid, she kept her away from her grandparents. Because who wanted role models like that in their daughter's life?"

It was a question I didn't need to answer, but one that forced me to think about what I would do in that position. To think about my future kid. If I ever had one. Would I have done the same?

I had no fucking idea. After what happened to my sister, I couldn't imagine God would make me be responsible for a child.

I would ruin him or her, too.

"Eventually Evie realized everything she'd lost, her daughter, her granddaughter, Peter ... And when she had enough and finally grew a backbone, she divorced Matt, but it was too late. Peter had already gotten married and had a family of his own.

"That's where the book comes in. Now Gertie spends her life alone, sitting on a park bench every day at 4:15pm, reading the happily ever after she never got. The alternate ending she always imagined."

Kate's shaky deep breath was heavy beside me. It was almost as if she were reliving the same life as the old woman on the park bench. I was afraid to look at her, to see her expression.

"If Evie would have just, for once, realized that the only way to be a true role model was to love herself first instead of deciding to stay was best for her daughter, she'd have the whole world right now."

"Kate," I said, my hand going to her thigh but stopping. I clutched the edge of the park bench instead. "Why are you telling me all this?"

"I don't know. Maybe because it's scary to be away from home, Ty, and I know how much you hate it here. Hell, the whole world can see that. But change is scary. Taking another road is scary, all the what-ifs and scenarios flooding your head. Or maybe it's okay to love two places like someone can love two people."

Kate inhaled, deep, dropping her hands on the bench on each side of her. Her hand brushed mine, but she didn't inch away. I stayed quiet, listening, soaking up her voice, her words, this story, and her reasoning.

"Or maybe I'm telling you all this because this city may be grand with all the flashy lights, good pizza, tall buildings, and secret hideaways. Everyone on the go, go, go, the hustle and bustle ... but if you pause for just a second and look around, you'll realize so much more. It's all a distraction."

She pulled a Sharpie from her purse, took my hand, and opened my palm. "It's the people, Ty," she said, and the wet, sticky ink was cold, but her eyes were warm. "I'm just one girl in this city, but it's all the people who make Manhattan. The homeless Veterans sleeping on subways and still wearing their hats proudly. A rapper stopping into a small record store just to make someone's day. The struggling shop owners selling their dreams for a pocket full of change. And the old woman on the bench who loved this city more than herself, ultimately sacrificing everything for it. This is New York. Passionate, intense, alive, fast, and manic," she said with finality.

I dropped my eyes to my palm.

Kate drew a black heart inside it.

"There are good people here who deserve a second chance. There's also good music inside you that these people need. And if you lost your heart somewhere along the way, all you have to do is retrace your steps."

Kate snapped the cap back on the marker and returned it to her bag. I hid the heart inside my closed fist and looked around.

A couple argued under a tree, their kids running around and between them, playing tag. Two men were making out on a bench to our right. A woman was breastfeeding her baby as her toddler fed the birds. Another woman in a business suit, cutting the air with a sadistic tone, shouting into her Bluetooth. It all made me feel entirely small at that moment.

But then my gaze fell back on her.

The sun lowered behind her, leaving the trees.

Kate wasn't just one girl in this city.

She was the entire city in one girl.

6:57 PM

S OMETHING CHANGED INSIDE ME. I FELT IT before leaving Central Park. Anger, grief, and confusion followed me all the way to thirty-eighth street in Midtown. The stadium full of emotions was overwhelming, clawing and scratching and beating inside me to escape. I was both drained by them and bouncing on my toes as we walked into a restaurant and down a flight of stairs.

The underground bar was like a study in someone's 1920's home. A speakeasy with velvet seating, antique lamps, and traditional burgundy rugs under our feet. There were built-in bookcases filled with books and liquor bottles used as bookends. Paintings that seemed to belong in the eighteenth century hung between dark wainscoted walls.

Kate led me to the corner of the bar, passing a man playing the piano on the way. For the next half hour, I sat next to a beautiful woman. A conversation that flowed easily distracted me from the black heart burning into my palm. For a short while, I'd forgotten what happened here six years ago.

"I'm treating you to dinner," Kate said after the waiter cleared empty appetizer plates from the table. I'd never let a woman treat me to dinner before, and it felt wrong to let her pay after everything I'd done, but she gave off an impression that she didn't take no for an answer.

"So why do it?" Kate asked after sipping from a tall glass of Veuve Clicquot Brut, and I circled my finger around the rim of my club soda and lime, knowing where this was going. "Why be in a relationship you don't want to be in? It doesn't make sense to me."

Her drinking liquor in front of me should have made me uneasy, but it didn't. I'd insisted she order what she wanted and didn't have to take my sweetened deal into consideration. I was also curious what Kate would be like with alcohol swimming inside her.

I picked up my drink and let it hover under my mouth. "Most things I do or am involved in wouldn't make sense to you. I wish I could explain it to you, but I can't."

"Because I won't understand?"

"Because of an NDA."

"Ah," Kate nodded, "It's complicated."

I tilted my head. "To put it lightly," I said and took a sip.

"Do you love her?"

"I do love her, yeah, but not in the way you're thinking. Gemma's been through a lot. *We've* been through a lot. I know the world makes her out to be this obnoxious and rude model at times, but she has good intentions ...." I paused, hearing myself talk about Gemma in a way that was so unexpected of me. "Gemma and I share something that only a few people can understand. I think it's why I'm impartial to her. To do anything she'd ask me to do. Maybe it doesn't make sense, but it's the only way I know how to explain it."

"You don't have to explain it to me, Ty."

"I get that, but I was so out of my mind earlier today. Like the world was pressing down on me, screaming in my fucking ear, and it took something crazy like—"

"Like kissing me?"

"Yeah," I smiled, "something crazy like kissing you, a stranger, in front of everyone, to get the noise to stop." My head rolled back before my eyes settled on hers again. "A second to just fucking breathe."

"What about music? Isn't that your outlet?"

"Music," I said, shaking my head. I was caught in the chase for so long, loyal to music like it were my wife. I'd given music my everything. I would have died for it, and in return, it took advantage of me. Betrayed me. Took away my freedom when it was supposed to drown me in it.

"Music was my outlet and love of my life for eighteen years. The industry has locks and chains, Kate, and music and I have been locked in a room together ever since. It suffocates me until I'm burning—*physically burning in my chest*—and now I resent it. I'm to the point where I want nothing to do with it. Music mocks me and laughs in my ears, and if it were a thing I could kill to make it stop, I would and never look back. It sounds stupid coming out of my mouth, but I'm still sitting here wondering how to escape music *and* learn to breathe without it. It's toxic." I closed my eyes and tried to calm the tremble in my hands. "Funny how that works, wanting to write off the only thing that keeps me alive .... One day, I'm afraid music and fame are going to bump fists and kill me, too."

It was the first time I admitted that out loud. Kate wasn't scared or gathering her things to take off. She didn't feel sorry for me or look at me with pity. Her reaction made me feel like I'd made sense and was normal. That I could trust her. And it was hard to trust anyone.

"When's the last time you made music for yourself? For fun?"

"It's been a long fucking time."

"Do you know how to play the piano?" Kate's gaze left me, and I followed it to see the piano in the corner of the room.

"Ah, I know where you're going with this. Don't hold your breath, Kate. It's not happening."

"We're just two random strangers in a random bar. I'm not asking you to play for me," she said, her hand on my thigh, the weight of the champagne charging all her actions. "I'm asking, for once, to let go and play, or rap, or whatever it is you feel like doing."

"I just confessed I wanted to murder music, and you want me to make love to it? Are you drunk right now?"

"A little," Kate said, leaning forward and holding up her thumb and finger, a small space between. "And I don't want you to make love to music, Ty. This is New York. I want you to fuck it."

My brows bounced, and a grin stretched across my face. It was a way to smother the nerves and tension building up inside me. "Wow. I've never heard you say fuck before, how did that feel?"

"Shut up and go face this bitch you've been locked in a room with. You're literally shaking just talking about. Like you have so much pent-up frustration. You need to take back control and show music what it's missing out on."

I was speechless. Pressured. Angry. And there was a purity of emotion and focus when you were angry.

I couldn't believe I was considering this.

"Go," Kate said, hands coming over my tats as she pushed my arm until I was standing.

I looked around, flattening my tee and adjusting the waistband of my jeans. Then I pointed at her with a foolish smile. It was a silencer to hide the gunshot of animosity. "This wasn't a part of the deal."

Kate lifted her champagne glass in the air. "Go breathe."

I walked across the room to the man playing the piano, asked him if I could have a moment with it.

He left me alone.

Just me and the piano and a mic.

I adjusted it, lowered it.

What came out of the tips of my fingers were keys to a beat I'd heard in my head since SoHo. Lyrics I'd written before but never left my lips. I wasn't nervous. My throat was scratchy and tight when I started to sing. Almost like it hadn't been used in a while. A foreign feeling, like returning to a place I hadn't visited in a long time.

The pain was intense, and there was a ferocity in my voice. The more I sang, everything else faded. The bar was a smokescreen, and at this moment, I was fighting an invisible enemy, pacing an invisible street, voice punctuating words, fingers punching keys. Deafening aggression burned a hole in the scene. Everything that I'd bottled up inside unraveled like slam poetry. All the frustration and anger and grief I'd held onto towards music boiled, burning me until I exploded into a pile of flesh and bones, blood spilling out into the bar.

I was nothing more than an open wound.

The chorus had come and gone, but I was too far gone to notice.

And by the time I finished, my hands fell from the keys, and my chest heaved for a solid breath. People in the underground bar cheered, clapped. But I was wasteland.

I looked at Kate, mad she did this to me and angrier at myself for letting her. She made me vulnerable. Exposed the ugly. We were on two opposite sides of the room, and she had her lips parted and a hand clutched to the center of her chest like she felt the same painful eruption that had happened inside of me.

But how could she?

It wasn't hers. It was all mine.

I spotted the stairs.

People began to approach the piano, and I took off, Nikes beating the solid wood before they could reach me.

DA
DUM

8:19 PM

I RAN OFF. AND IF MUSIC WAS MY EX, THEN THE street was a stripper. City lights bounced and beamed, poking its claws into the night. But it was hot. Bold, blistering, and heavy as a daytime summer sky.

My palms hit the front siding of the building, and I leaned over, dropping my head against the paned windows. I chugged the polluted air as if it were a bottle of Vodka. Whiskey. Anything but club soda and lime and heartache.

If I hadn't made this deal with Kate, I'd be on my way to any number of nightclub hotspots. I would already be drunk with a numb and dumb smile, not dealing with confronting my painstaking past.

It was the song. It was Kate. It was this whole damn city.

I clenched my fist and pulled back, ready to punch through the glass storefront.

But something stopped me.

My fist locked inside another.

It was Kate, and her hand came over my forearm, turning me around.

My arms instantly wrapped around her. My face hid in her hair. She held me tight, and for a while, we stayed still like a broken clock while the fast-paced city and nightlife ticked around us.

I knew we cried from our eyes. It was something our bodies did and not something we had to think about. It just happened. Though I couldn't force the tears out, I could stop them from coming. But with my jaw tight and teeth clenched, it felt like the rest of my body was crying. Emotional. Weeping. Breathing.

"Ty Hendrix? Oh my gosh, Tyler Hendrix!"

The timing was awful. It always was.

I released Kate, clearing my throat, looking up, and wiping my arm across my forehead. "Yeah, hey."

The transition happened so easily, so quickly. Bottling myself so that no one could see. They expected my attention. They expected me to drop everything I was doing, everything I'd been feeling, and give them a hundred percent like I owed them something because they downloaded my music. Why would Ty Hendrix brush me off if I was a number in his net worth?

Two girls had phones pulled out, cameras on and facing me.

Another group of girls trailed behind, coming at us.

"Where's Gemma?" one asked, side-eyeing Kate.

Kate.

I flicked my eyes to Kate, my hands moving on autopilot and signing things that had been thrown my way. Kate had taken steps back, clutching her purse close to her side. The crowd was growing, and she distanced herself. Good.

"Who is that?" another girl asked. "I'd never seen her before."

I looked back at the growing group of girls and shrugged. "I don't know, just a girl, but I have to get going ... Okay, one more picture."

"When's your next album coming? We've been waiting forever!"

"Don't know." It was the same response every time. Even if I were to drop anything, why give them enough time to form an opinion about it or make assumptions on what to expect?

Just when I broke away from the crowd, Kate was gone.

My heart slammed in my chest.

I gazed up and down the busy street. Cars honked, and music thumped from cracked windows. I patted my pocket for my phone, then realized I didn't have it. It would have been useless anyway. I didn't have Kate's number, either.

I was stranded and alone in a city I hated.

I had no idea where Kate could have run off to or why she'd run off at all. I recognized the irony. It was the same way I'd fled my problems, racing to alcohol and sex and anything else that could come between music and me to make me forget. I could create my own versions of heaven under the influence. But now I was sober and wandering along Thirty-sixth Street, and the city had eyes that followed me, skyscrapers with chainsaws and other things with teeth.

I didn't know how long I'd been walking for. It felt like hours.

To my right, the top of the Empire State building stabbed the sky, hid the same stars that I was sure shone brightly on the west coast. Could I spot Kate from the top? Was she on her way back to SoHo, riding the subway alone? I retraced our steps, our day.

That was when it hit me, and I looked down at the center of my palm where Kate had left a black heart inside.

I knew where she was.

The night was quiet here. No laughing, no screaming.

I found Kate sitting on the same green bench, this time with two vintage suitcases—stickers of various countries peeling and scattering across the front—resting on the ground at her feet. She was the loudest thing in the park, sitting alone with her arms crossed and looking up at the moonlight between the trees like a public service announcement. She was beautiful, though, even with her horrible taste in shoes.

Her head lowered, and she settled her eyes on me.

I felt her gaze hit my spine. Was she upset about what I said about her on the sidewalk in front of the mob of girls? I couldn't tell. *Fuck*, I couldn't tell.

I couldn't remember exactly what I'd said about her, either. "I'm sorry for whatever I said back there. I didn't mean it, and it's safer that way. You have to believe me."

Kate didn't say anything. She just sat there and looked at me, her big blue eyes like nails and reaching into the depths of my soul. I couldn't escape the confrontation this time. Our twelve hours were almost up, and Kate wanted the answer to the one question I'd been avoiding for six years.

"You may be some stranger I kissed on the sidewalk, but I wouldn't go as far as dragging you into my shitty life if I can help it. Yeah, what I did was stupid, but I'll keep you far away from it all if I can because this city, music, it all broke my fucking heart once already. I'm not strong enough to endure it a second time."

"I know," she said. "I know what happened."

"No, you don't know. You only know what the media tells you."

Water shook in her eyes when she said, "You lost your girlfriend and your sister in one night. I'll never forget that. *No one* will ever forget that."

"I didn't *lose* my sister, Kate," I spat. "I didn't misplace her like I would a set of keys, she didn't go missing. She's dead, and it's because of me." My vision blurred with my statement, a dizziness, a weakness. It was the way she'd said *lose* out loud and clear when the truth has been whispering in my ears ever since. *You killed your sister.*

"The girl I was with? Lana? It was never anything serious. She was just a fling. Some model I was fucking at the time ... and she was Gemma's best friend. If I thought for one second that some crazy and obsessed fan would go as far as shooting her, I would have never put her in that position. And I didn't think one bullet could kill two people, either. I didn't think one bullet could take out Lana *and* Tanya."

"Ty, I'm so sorry ..." Kate said, a single tear on the loose and running down her cheek. Then another one. "I didn't mean it like that."

She was a mirror of my inner child that was never really gone. A time when I believed the world was up for the taking and nothing bad would ever happen—a time when it was okay to cry when things hurt and hide when life got scary.

Self-pity looked good on no one, and her single tear set me off, resurrected the rage.

She was crying for me, and I didn't deserve it.

Looking down at her, my hands shook. I fisted them to make it stop. "Yeah, well, I'm sorry, too, because Tanya and Lana didn't ask for this. My sister was young—only sixteen with her whole life ahead of her. The fame was supposed to take me too soon, not her. Not fucking her!" I turned into a pile of anger and spit and oral ammo, firing at her as if she were the piano.

I gripped the back of my neck and turned around.

"I'm right here," I heard her say behind me. "You don't have to hide. Please, just tell me what happened. I want to know what happened. But from you this time."

It was a scene that replayed in my head for six years, blocking the beat I once had. "Tanya just came to the show because it's fucking New York," I continued, turning back around with my arms up at my sides. "But I never thought anything like this could happen. The things I screamed that night at the crazy girl, taking her down and punching her in the face *over* and *over* again, I was just ... Fuck, she just shot my sister, Kate. My sister was dead, I wasn't thinking straight, and I didn't know what to do. She could have shot me, why Tanya and Lana? Why did *my* sister have to die?"

"Olivia Davis."

My eyes snapped to her. "What?"

"You haven't said her name," Kate said through her tears. "You've said everyone else's name but the girl who shot Tanya, Lana, and herself. Her name was Olivia Davis. I'm not saying this to take away from what happened to your friend and sister, but three girls died that night, Ty. And the most twisted part is that while they dedicate a ceremony to Tanya and Lana every year, the whole world forgot about Olivia. She wasn't mentally stable. She was sick and never got the help she needed. You can't blame your fans, you can't blame New York, you can't blame music, you can't blame Olivia, and you can't blame yourself. What happened is horrible, but if you keep transferring blame, you'll never find peace with what happened."

"Olivia." It felt like a curse word leaving my mouth. Olivia killed my sister, and I hated myself for thinking all these years that I was glad she was dead, too. That because her parents never got her help, now they had to live with the pain I had to live with. Kate was right, and these guilty thoughts simmered inside me as she watched me from below.

"Is that why you and Gemma are close? Because she was there with you and witnessed her best friend dying?"

I nodded. "No one but her will understand what happened that night after the concert, but the craziest part about it all, even though I haven't come out with an album since, I'm even more famous because of it. Tell me how sick and fucked up that is. If I could go back to being a nobody so I could keep my sister, I'd do it in a heartbeat. Fuck the label. Fuck the music. Fuck the fame. I never wanted it anyway. I never gave a fuck about the status or streams or numbers. Fuck everything. It's not worth it. The only reason I'm here and stuck in this contract is because Gemma needed this movie debut to go well. And yeah, I owed her that much after a fan of mine took her best friend. But you know what? My sister died, too. If I had just—"

Kate started to shake her head. "Ty, this—"

"Nah, stop. I already know what you're going to say, but it doesn't make the pain stop. I heard you, I know it's not my fault. I know there was nothing I could do. I've heard it all before, but my chest, my head, it all still fucking hurts. And after today, I realize all this now more than ever."

I went silent, shoulders rising and falling, and dropped my head back to catch my breath. Kate remained silent, too, and I felt her eyes on me.

"Tanya," I whispered as if she were here, then squeezed the bridge of her nose before returning my eyes to Kate to lift the heaviness in me. "She always dreamed of coming here. I couldn't get her to shut up about it. And seeing the city through your eyes today reminded me of that day before she died when the city reflected in her's. I get it now, Kate. I do. I've been wasting my time blaming New York when I should be experiencing it for her. I should have been making music through the pain this whole time instead of avoiding it. I know. I may not have it all figured out, but I'm finally catching on."

It had been a long time since I let Kate talk. I took a step closer with my hands in my pockets. "That's why I asked for twelve hours with you. Because it only took twelve hours the last time in New York before my sister was gone. Maybe twelve hours more would bring her back. And in a way, it did."

Kate's cheeks were glossy on both sides of her small smile. "I'm happy you kissed me on the sidewalk today, Ty. Maybe the universe has a way of bringing two strangers together in desperate times."

It wasn't until after some time had passed when I caught myself smiling back, then shook my head and dropped my gaze to the suitcases. "So, what's with the luggage? Are you cutting our time short and taking off? Wasn't going to bother to say goodbye?"

Kate's breath came out shaky on an exhale like she was still recovering from my emotional lashing. "I have an hour left, and there's one more stop we have to make." She stood, leaned forward, and grabbed the handle of each suitcase. "Are you okay?"

I took a suitcase from her, knowing it was best to not ask questions. "Yeah, I'm okay."

2:43 AM

WE FACED THE BEAUTIFUL ARC WINDOWS OF Grand Central Station. The suitcase handle was sweaty in my palm, and I tightened my fist, adjusted my grip. "What are we doing here?"

Kate's attention remained on the clock in the middle of the station. It was almost two-forty-five in the morning. "C'mon. We don't have much time."

I followed her down a flight of steps to the lower concourse until we reached ground level.

"Stay here," Kate said. Then she walked until she was on the opposite end of the same arc.

She said my name, and though she was more than ten feet away, her voice was in my ear as if she were standing right next to me. "Can you hear me?"

Bodies breezed between us, people coming and going. How could I hear her?

"Ty," she said again. "Look at me." My eyes snapped back to hers, and it felt as if my intestines were tying in knots. Kate's smile managed to calm me, to focus me. "This is it. We're leaving our guilt trapped inside these suitcases, leaving them at the station, and never looking back."

"How can I hear you right now when you're so far away?"

She laughed. "You don't have to shout. Just talk normally and focus. The arch will carry your voice to me."

I coughed into my fist. "Okay, okay."

"What I have to say isn't nearly as gut-wrenching as what you told me, but I made a promise to you. I told you that if you told me about why you hated New York, I'd tell you about the boots." Her expression was a mixture of embarrassment, awkwardness, and sadness.

"Pain isn't a competition, Kate." I adjusted the handle of the suitcase in my hand, wanting to stand in front of her and not ten feet away. "How deep or brutal our scars are in comparison isn't the fucking point. It's not like that. And the fact you waited until now to finally tell me shows me you listened and cared. You could have just told me about the boots back at Central Park, but you didn't. Because it would have taken away from my sister, from me. You gave me time, were there with me. You didn't spin some bullshit about losing someone, too. I'm not an idiot, everyone's lost someone. But you didn't take what I said and make it about you." I dropped my chin, felt a smile creep along my lips, then looked back up at her. "You're a good woman, Kate."

"It just seems so juvenile telling you this after what you told me."

"It matters. It's a part of you, right?" I shrugged. "I want to hear, and you still have to leave something behind in that suitcase. I'm not doing this alone."

Kate took a second to gather her thoughts, and I gave it to her, neither one of us moving from our side of the arc.

"Okay, so my mom and I never had much growing up. She ran away from New York as soon as possible to get away from her parents, then had me. It was always just us two, and life with her meant city to city, man to man, trailer park to trailer park, making ends meet. I never really had anything but these stories she used to tell me about this amazing city where dreams were born. We only bought what we needed, and it was always enough. I was okay with it until I grew up and needed more. I realized I couldn't go on without knowing what couch I was going to sleep on the next day. What town I'd end up in. I couldn't take it anymore. As soon as I turned eighteen, I left and managed to get here with only twenty bucks." She laughed. "Pocket change, Ty. I worked my ass off, and every day I walked past those boots on my way to work. Not at the coffee shop, I didn't have it then, but at this elite restaurant. Seeing those boots in the window every day kept me moving forward when the lights went out, or on days I couldn't eat."

"Well, you chose an expensive city."

"Tell me about it, but I was determined to buy those boots when everything else failed me. To me, they represented so much more than boots. A home, a future. I was determined to make something of myself, no matter how hard it got. I moved up fast, became manager, saved a crapload of money to buy the store in SoHo. And when I made the first hundred bucks, I went back to the window for those damn boots, but they were gone."

"Damn, life is a bully. Sometimes I think it enjoys fucking with our lives."

Kate nodded. "It took me six months to find them. They were out of season, but I never gave up." She laughed until it faded. "It's funny, really. My mom ran away from New York because she didn't want the city holding her back like it did for her mom, Gertie. I ran back to it for the same reason. To let a place hug me so tight, I couldn't breathe. A place to call home." She shrugged. "This place is what we make it, Ty. We can either let the city hold us so tight until we can't breathe, or we can allow it to let us go."

"Wait. Gertie Ellis? That whole story in the park ... That woman is your grandmother?"

"Yeah. Gertie's my grandmother, but she doesn't know me. Not yet."

The way I felt for Kate increased to new limits with her confession. Growing up, I'd always had Linc and Tanya and a place to run back to when things got hard. Kate had no one until she found her way back here. At one point in time, Kate and I were on two different spectrums. She was once the hungry girl with stars in her eyes, who would have sold her soul to get where she was today, and I was once the rap god who took everything for granted.

Today, we'd crossed paths when we both needed it the most: when she was about to lose her restaurant, and I was about to lose myself.

Kate was right. Maybe the universe did know when to bring two total strangers together in desperate times. And our timing couldn't have been more perfect.

With her, I was hearing music again.

"Drop your suitcase, Ty. It's time to let go."

My knees bent, and I let the suitcase go along with everything that had been weighing me down. Kate did the same, and when I straightened my spine, the heaviness floated off me.

The clock struck three AM.

Kate and I peeled our eyes away from the marquee and settled them on each other. The way she looked at me had my heart punching out of my chest. She'd seen more of me in twelve hours than anyone had in six years, and she stayed. We'd gone this far, and there was nothing more to hold us back.

"I want to fuck you," I said.

A woman stopped in her tracks, turned to face me. "Excuse me, young man?"

"No, ma'am. Not you. That wasn't for you." A laugh burst from the other side of the arc, and Kate's hand came over her mouth to stifle a giggle. "Her," I said. "I want to fuck her."

The old woman grimaced before turning and walking away, the wheels on her luggage spinning behind her. Kate's cheeks flushed a crimson-red.

I took a step toward her. "Kate."

"Ty."

We met in the middle of the arc.

3:03 AM

I RACED BEHIND KATE TO THE SIX SUBWAY BACK TO SoHo before it took off. It was the last train of the night, and we hopped on before the doors closed.

Kate gripped the back of my head, fisting my shirt and pinning her body to mine. My mouth came down on hers, fast and open and greedy to taste her again. When our tongues collided, brushed, touched, it was blood-pumping and enough to lose my mind.

"I knew it," a man yelled.

Kate pulled away from me, her breath staggering and dragging across my lips. I opened my eyes and turned my head. It was the homeless man.

"Thatta boy, she gonna sit on your face."

Kate's giggle was infectious. She grabbed my hand, yanking me down the middle aisle and through doors to another train car. The sound of the train against the track was like a heartbeat. Paced and steady against our mania.

Her blonde hair twirled when she turned back to look at me with a wicked smile. One that caused my cock to jump and my heart to get clogged in my throat.

It was illegal to jump cars, there were signs on the wall saying as much, but at this hour, we were lawless lovers chasing the night.

We stopped running once we reached an empty car, and Kate fell into my arms. Her hands clung to my neck, and I dipped down to kiss her once more, stroking her tongue with mine. The cherry taste made me weak, and I gripped her hips and took her backward with me until we fell onto a beaten seat.

Kate stood between my spread knees.

I looked up at her, and her eyes admired me in a way that hadn't before. I splayed my fingers across her naked thighs, gripped the backs of them. Kate didn't look away, lids hooded, eyes drenched. She fisted the hem of her skirt and lifted it, revealing panties that had a music note stitched on the front.

My heart slammed in my chest, and I inched my fingers higher and *higher* and hooked her panties, sliding them down until they rolled off the heels of her cowboy boots. I shoved them deep in my pocket and stared at her perfect bare pussy, my eyes worshipping it.

Kate's eyes turned heavy, and she wet her lips as goosebumps spread across her skin. She lifted her leg and planted a boot on the seat beside me, her pink pussy spread like an offering. Like

I paid for this. Like I deserved this. Whatever I wanted. My words caught in my throat. I was drunk from the sight. My dick throbbed to be inside her. To taste her.

My fingertips grazed her soaked slit, her opening, her pink lips. Gentle at first. Kate fisted the hem of her skirt as I explored, swaying against my touch, and the way she moved with me was intoxicating. All the blood in my body free fell and rushed to my cock.

I watched her features as I slid a finger inside her tight hole. Kate's lashes fluttered, and her pussy clamped around my finger. The room spun, hazy and high on her. I pulled my finger out and licked her juices off before dipping two back inside her. The sweetness was addicting and never enough.

Kate let go of her skirt, and the material fell around my arm. She was touching her neck, her hair, her head rolling back as I pumped into her. My midnight angel was so fucking sexy, and I couldn't take it anymore. I pulled out, flipped my hat around, and gripped her ass with both hands. Yanking her forward, I took her entire pussy into my mouth.

My tongue glided through the sweet center, and Kate melted against my face. I caught her hips, sinking my flat tongue inside her entrance, pressing with precise long licks, sliding in and out. Kate grabbed the back of my head and rolled her hips into my mouth with a cry I could get off from.

My whole body felt light, and my cock felt heavy, stretched, and hard against my sweats. One touch, and I was afraid to explode without ever being inside her.

I clamped down on her pussy, my teeth scraping her clit, my tongue flicking her entrance. She was watching me from above.

Our gazes locked, and Kate dug her teeth into her bottom lip just before her mouth fell open.

She whimpered and tried to pull away, tried to cover my head with her skirt, but I squeezed her ass and yanked her forward. I used both thumbs to stretch and massage her opening from behind and thrust my tongue deep inside.

Kate's expression melted when the orgasm hit like an explosion. Her beautiful, tanned legs shook as she tried to hold herself together. She gripped a nearby pole, and I moved a palm over her pubic bone and pulled up, spreading her open and kneading her clit with my thumb until she came in my mouth, cum on my tongue and pussy beating against my lips.

My hands left her to drop my sweats. Fast. My ready and thick cock jumped out, and I fisted the base, hooked an arm around her, and pulled her close until she was straddling me. She hovered my thick head, dripping on it.

"Ah, Fuck, Kate," I said from the sight. Kate whimpered in response, desperately eager to be filled. I grabbed the space between her thighs to stop her, to tell her something, and my balls tightened at the warm and soaked pussy in the palm of my hand. "When tomorrow comes, don't you dare forget about me."

Kate's dancing blue eyes narrowed. "Then make sure you fuck me so good, you leave an impression, Ty Hendrix."

I sucked on my lips to hide my smile and cupped her neck with one hand. Then plunged my cock deep inside her.

Kate's jaw fell open, and my palm moved down the length of her neck. "God, you're fucking perfect."

Her heat and tightness fisted my cock, and I could have come right then, but the feel of her paralyzed me, sent me into a shock.

I had her pinned down—my cock deep and to the hilt—and grabbed her thighs to keep her in a slow grind. I wanted to stay connected to her like this for as long as possible. To plant myself, grow roots and never leave.

I kissed her neck to slow time. The taste of her delicate skin could inspire me, and the touch of the cold metal of her earring on my lips shot a shiver to my brain like a hit of menthol.

The train car stopped, and the doors slid open, but we were in too deep. Someone could get on, and I wouldn't notice. The world would have to fight me. The world would have to slit my throat to pull her away from me. The thought was painful yet equally exhilarating, knowing someone could see us like this. The Ty and Kate show. The thrill of it all spurred me on.

The doors closed, and with my lips paused on her neck, I chanced a look around to see that we were all alone.

Kate's mouth caught mine, and she balled my shirt in her fists, the two of us succumbing to each other in every way possible. One hand fisted her hair, the other squeezed her ass. The tip of my finger pressed against her tight little asshole, and my tongue swept across hers, praising her and urging her to never stop. My moans tumbled down her throat as her pussy walls squeezed my dick every time she rolled her hips.

We were a track of hearts pounding and heavy breathing. Lights bounced in the tunnel, shining bright before fading out.

"Oh my God, Ty," Kate cried in my ear, the next orgasm coming with a warning and spreading across her hot skin, her sweaty palms trying to find grip.

I slammed inside her once more. "Stand up," I ordered, and Kate looked at me with despair as her thighs shook.

I tossed her up onto her feet.

My sweats dropped to my ankles as I turned and bent her over the bench. *The art you create is immortal* was tattooed on the base of her spine, and I knew I'd seen those words before. I squeezed my eyes closed and opened them again, then wrapped my arm around her hip until my long fingers were gliding through her pussy lips.

"Part your legs and find balance," I whispered in her ear while my middle finger stroked her swollen clit, the same thing she'd told me the last time we were on the subway. I flipped up her skirt, and her bare ass was decorated and red from my hands.

My heavy cock pulsed, ready to unload, and I watched myself slowly inch back inside her to feel everything all over again.

My slow grind turned into a pounding, but my fingers continued the slow graze on her clit. I pulled down her shirt with my free hand and slid my fingers across her chest until I cupped her warm and naked breast. Her hard nipple rolled between my fingers, and my entire body clenched like she had a full, invisible grip on my being.

Then the beat was in my ears. Loud. Slamming. Hard. Vibrating my bones until we both exploded.

I didn't think about pulling out. Not once. I pinned my gaze to Kate's expression, eyes squeezed shut, hair stuck to her cheek, as I came inside her, and she coated me.

I only pulled out because her legs were shaking, unable to stand anymore. Evidence of our climaxes dripped down her thigh when I collapsed onto the bench, taking her with me.

Then everything heavy left Kate's body. She was nothing more than a pile of mush in my arms. Her forehead fell onto my shoulder, and I wrapped my arms around her and kissed her temple.

Our chests heaved against each other.

Sweat slid down the edges of my hairline.

And we laughed as the train came to a halt at our stop.

3:26 AM

THE TWO OF US TOOK OUR TIME BACK TO THE SOHO Grand Hotel. Though we were quiet with our fingers laced and bodies wasted, we were content. I was happy. Kate, somehow, was everything I'd needed. The city, somehow, was more vibrant, and, if it were at all possible, my senses were more alive. There was an abundance of warring emotion bubbling up inside me, too. My fingers itched to write. To produce. To call Colorado and book the studio for tomorrow to let it all out to prolong this feeling. Ride it out for as long as possible.

However, when we reached the entrance to the hotel, there was also tightness in my chest. A clawing that only dug deeper. I turned Kate toward me, and she took off my shades to see my face.

My gaze swept across the sidewalk, the street, before it settled back on her.

Her smile beamed, cheeks flushed and glowing. "So, I guess this is where we go our separate ways."

I gripped her hand in mine. "We don't have to." I didn't want this night to end. I wasn't ready to let the beat go. Kate's panties were burning a hole in my pocket, and I didn't want that to be the only thing I had left of her. I wanted more than fucking panties. I didn't know exactly what I wanted, just more.

"C'mon, Kate. This doesn't have to be the end. Stay the night."

"I can't."

"You can't?" I laughed an empty laugh, pulling her closer and rubbing my thumb across hers, "and why not? Do you have a boyfriend you have to go home to or something? because I really don't give a fuck if you do."

Her hand slipped from my fingers. "It was always about music just as much as it was about New York. I hope you fall in love again with both this time, Ty."

"Stop." I rolled my eyes. "My checkbook is upstairs. Let me at least hold up my end of the bargain. Let me help you save your restaurant."

"After we did what we did? No way, I'm not a hooker," she said, shaking her head and pulling away from me with a laugh I couldn't decipher.

I grabbed her arm and spun her back around, standing before her again. "Wait. Just slow down a second. Are you upset?"

Kate's shoulders slumped, and a lazy smile spread across her lips. "No. I'm the opposite of upset. I'm happy. Let's not ruin it with money or deals or anything else. It always destroys things, doesn't it? Let's just end it here while we're both in this place, okay?"

"Okay," I said, lying through my fucking teeth. It wasn't okay. I wasn't going to let Kate lose her restaurant. If I had no other choice, I'd find another way to save it. "We'll not ruin it, but it's not the end of us, Kate," I said, sliding my hand down her arm to pull her closer to me. "The universe will make sure of that."

I took off her hat and pushed her hair back until she was looking up at me.

"Don't forget, Ty. Pay no attention to what everyone else is doing. If you fall, get right back up. And write with honesty."

There was a tempo in her eyes when she'd said it.

Then I understood. I'd understood it all.

It was the three rules she'd told me on the subway, but it was about the music all along.

I kissed her one last time on the sidewalk.

I kissed her so deeply, it felt like she was vanishing in my arms.

But this time, I was kissing her in the middle of the night as the vibrant spirit of New York—everything that Tanya had fallen in love with that I didn't until now—rushed around us.

SOMETIMES THE CITY MADE MUSIC, AND sometimes it made noise. But on this day, the commotion streamed through my ears and into my head. It was a hellish feeling. I wished it would go away.

Still, the light was bright. The air was fresh.

SoHo was alive, just as I was.

Clouds drifted beneath my feet, and the pounding in my head was out of beat. Out of focus and everything off-kilter. It sucked me in, spat me out, and I was right back to where I'd been all along: laying on the sidewalk with the sultry sun crawling higher and beating against my face.

Car horns blared, and the trap music playing from cracked windows drowned out Gemma's cries.

I opened my eyes, and the sun weaved between the crowd of people standing over me, their faces a blur. I rubbed my eyes.

"His eyes are open!" Gemma cried into the phone glued to her ear, black mascara streaming down her face. I noticed that much.

"Lay back down, sir. An ambulance is on the way," someone else said.

Get the fuck away from me, I thought, but my mouth wasn't moving. My voice was trapped in my head. I sat up and turned to the side. A puddle of blood was next to me.

Someone ordered the crowd to back up and give me some room. People threw opinions and directions like they knew what was best for me.

Angry, I jumped to my feet, touched my head, and looked at my fingers. The blood was sticky and thick. "What happened?"

"Did you take something? Pills?" Gemma cried through her whisper, my eyes trying to focus and piece her face back together. "You blacked out, Ty. I was so scared. You just slumped out of your chair and hit the ground. It all happened so fast, and I couldn't get to you in time."

"You've been unresponsive for a minute," someone else said, and I heard his voice but couldn't see his face. I knew I didn't know him. I didn't know any of these people.

Gemma handed me my glasses, and I slipped them on. Everything was clear again. Chaos crowded me, and I pushed them out of the way. My brain pounded in my skull as I looked around, seeing nothing but worried eyes, the back of a hundred or more phones facing me. I dropped my head and pressed against my temples, trying to stop the street from spinning.

When I glanced up, blood trickled into my eyes, and a bright light blinded me, bounced off my glasses. I wiped the corners of my eyes and raked my fingers through my hair, looking back to see where it had come from.

Across the cobblestone street, a waitress wearing a crisp white button-up and black tie was looking right at me. A serving tray dangled from her fingertips at her side. Her hair was pulled back in a ponytail, blonde strands framing her face. *Kate.* I took a step onto the cobblestone street. A car screeched, braking just in time, but I didn't bother moving out of the way. I pounded my fist on the hood and kept walking. "Kate!"

"Ty, where are you going? Come back!" Gemma shouted over the chatter. Cameras swarmed all around, paparazzi clicking away.

"Ty Hendrix," another man called out. "You should sit down. You shouldn't be walking."

My attention never left Kate, and I didn't stop until she was in front of me. I felt every crevice of the cobblestone street under my Nikes on the way. I was lightheaded but consumed by a newfound inspiration. Enough of it to spill out of me.

Kate's eyes went wide when I approached.

The freckle was gone, and her eyes were no longer blue but a greenish hazel. I looked down, and the heart she drew in my palm was no longer there. None of it made sense.

"Kate?" I took a step back, wiping my forehead with my arm.

The tray dropped from her fingers when I said her name. It spun on the sidewalk until it laid flat next to her shoes. They weren't leather or boots but basic white sneakers. *This is wrong*, I thought. The story about the boots slammed into me, made me question my thoughts and everything that led to this moment.

Then my gaze drifted up her body when it hit her nametag.

Kate was printed on her breast pocket, and a sigh left my lips.

I erased the small distance and grabbed the back of her head. And I kissed her.

The moment our lips touched, Kate pulled away and raised a hand to slap me, but I caught it in my fist.

"I know you better than that."

"What are you doing?" she whispered, trying to take her hand back. "You don't know me at all."

"Yes. Yes, I do," I said. Kate was the girl who liked a *mad good* slice of pizza and knew every word to an Eminem song. I took the hand she had slapped me with once upon a time and laced my fingers with hers.

Then I felt something that wasn't supposed to be there.

I dropped my head, examined her hand, stared at it.

"And what if I was married?"

"Are you?"

"I could be. What if I was married, and you just kissed me like you did. You really should think before you act, Ty...."

I looked up at her, feeling all the color leave my face. "You're married?" I squeezed her hand, not wanting to let it go. *Am I dead? What if this is what Hell feels like?* "How are you married? I don't understand."

Kate took back her hand and narrowed her eyes.

She was good at that.

"Yes, I'm married. You don't understand because you don't know me," she reiterated.

We stood in a silent standoff, neither of us breaking away from the hold. The longer we stood there, confusion raking my core, the more something was breaking inside Kate. I didn't know what it was, but I saw the moment it happened in her eyes.

It looked like an Empire state of mind.

"It's the universe, Kate."

I'd witnessed a bucket full of things in her eyes before—anger, admiration, music—but this time it was a sense of power breaking out of chains and slavery leaving her irises. Freedom, fire, and full of intensity. They were aimed at me, hammering out decisions between blinks.

I took a step closer, wrapping my fingers around her wrist. The *click, click, click* from the cameras became background noise.

I rubbed my thumb across hers. "You were once the music, weren't you?"

Kate looked around at the crowd, and I placed the tips of my fingers on her jawline to direct her eyes back to me.

Then she fisted my shirt and pulled me down until our mouths crashed.

Passionate, intense, alive, fast, and manic like the city.

IN TOO DEEP

NICOLE FIORINA

To read more about Ty & Kate, make sure you stay up to date with me by following me on Instagram or signing up for my newsletter at nicolefiorina.com

NOTE FROM AUTHOR

I've never been a drinker. Maybe twice a month, at most. Growing up, I've experimented with drugs, but never the hard stuff. Mary-Jane and Molly were fleeting friends. When you know you have an addictive personality, and grew up fighting off other people's demons, you choose what you want to stick around after peer pressure and experimenting. Like me, some have the mindset of *I refuse to be anything like my mother or father or sister or brother and etc...* because if you don't, you'll end up being *just* like them. It's one extreme or the other. I never wanted to be like them, so my steadfast self was my savior. Until five years ago.

I was in a car accident that left me temporarily disabled and restricted to a bed for about six months. During that time, I took pills to ease the pain. The prescription was easier than getting stabbed with needles in the neck and lower back weekly by doctors I didn't know to help with pain that only returned again and again. At first, I was hesitant with painkillers because I've watched family members go down that dark path, but the constant suffering was unbearable, and I couldn't handle the shots anymore. They felt like a violation, and my anxiety of being touched was eating away at me piece by piece. *The pills were for the pain,* I convinced myself. *I can control the intake. I got this. I'm not like this person or that one. I'm Nicole, and I have this under control.* So, I stopped the shots and took the pills.

One weekend, after being in bed for a long six months, I left the house for a family cook-out. It was summer, and Florida's summers feel like the sun is a giant fist being shoved down your throat while rays are slapping your skin. I knew what was coming, so I took more painkillers that I should have that day. I just wanted to have a good, old-fashioned time and didn't want to spend those few hours with my family thinking about the pain. I remember sitting on the back patio. Everyone was there: Christian, Gracie, Michael, my nieces and nephews, my sisters, Mom, and her husband. The kids just got out of the pool and were eating in front of the TV. The adults sat around patio arguing about something stupid because we're a loud, competitive Italian family. I remember talking to one of my sisters about a struggle she was having with a boy. Apparently, that's when I dropped.

Then I was at a rock concert. It doesn't make sense, I know that as I'm typing, but this happened. I was at a rock concert, and my dad was there. He passed away nine years prior, so seeing him was like a soul squeeze. My heart was in a tight fist.

I remember being happy. The kind of happiness that fills your entire body with a lightness that lifts you up so high and makes you want to cry. I knew of Michael and my two beautiful children who were waiting for me at my mom's house, but I had no desire to go back. I wanted to stay right where I was and head-bang to live rock with my dad in the dark under the constant moving lights. I remembered it being strange that I didn't worry about my kids, which I do whenever they're not with me, but somehow, I knew they were okay. I remembered the pain, both physical and mental, but I was at peace. I never wanted to leave this place.

Something pulled me back, and when I came to, I was across the yard, folded in half over Michael's arm with his fingers down my throat. I wasn't at a rock concert anymore, and as gut-wrenching as it feels to type this, I wasn't with my dad anymore either.

I still don't know what happened to me. I don't know if it was a dream, heaven, or some alternate reality my brain conjured to hold me while unconscious. I don't know, but I'll never forget the few minutes passing that felt like hours in front of a stage next to my dad with a smile that still burns my cheeks to this day. The kids never witnessed their mom or aunt in that state, but whatever the state was, ended up pushing me to get my ass out of bed. I healed faster, stopped the pills, took care of myself, and got back to writing and fell in love with it all over again. And if you believe in the unexplainable like I do, I would like to think my dad—in a way—gifted me a reality check from beyond.

What If has been on my mind ever since.

Tyler Hendrix, an artist who took too many painkillers on the sidewalk before creating his alternate reality, his dream, his heaven, whatever he needed it to be. The ending of this short story isn't for everyone, but it's left in a place that feels right to me.

I never intended for this to be a full-length novel, but I grew attached to these two characters and need to see how this love story plays out.

Until then, the core is still here. Ty awoke from his daydream with the love of music again. A force re-born inside him that was passionate, intense, alive, fast, and manic like the city of dreams. And maybe Kate *was* the music all along.

At least for now.

Xoxo,
nicole

THANK YOU

Thank you for taking the time to read Ty and Kate's short story. This is only the beginning of their love story, but you are now a part of their world, and I couldn't be happier.

Thank you to the women with Beyond the Read and those who were part of Beyond the Love anthology, What If's original home. Especially **Amanda Shephard** and **Mercedes Velez**. It's these two who motivated me to write this story at this time in my life, and if it weren't for you guys, I don't know if I'd ever have the guts to go through with it. So much love for the both of you!

Thank you to **Ashlee O'Brien** with Ashes & Vellichor, the designer for everything Ty & Kate, including the gorgeous covers. I adore the connection we have and so happy that I found a designer who truly knows and understands my vision, aesthetic, and brand. I love you to Washington and back.

Kassy Dosal (K Dosal), thank you for our beautiful and real friendship, for always being the first to read my work, and always looking out for me. Forever and ever. xoxo

To my team, **Krysten & Katie**! Thank you for all you do so I can continue writing these stories. I love you ladies and so lucky to have you both!

Julia Ponce, I'm so grateful to have you in my life and cherish this bond we have. Thank you for beta reading the beginning of Ty and Kate's story and always giving me honest feedback. Love you!

To my husband, **Michael**: when it comes to me, you always jump first, ask questions later. Thank you for trusting me and risking it all for NFB and our family. I love you. I love us.

To my **Street Team, the NF Gang, and my readers** around the globe: thank you for always trusting in me, for believing in me, for always taking a chance on my art no matter which direction I take. I love and appreciate each and every one of you.

MORE BY NICOLE FIORINA

STAY WITH ME TRILOGY

This trilogy is for the **poetry lovers**, dreamers, and those who love emotional rollercoasters and suspense. Mia and Ollie's love story is known to be a tear-jerker, with dark, broken, and beautiful themes (#passthetissues). All three books are complete and available for free on Amazon's KindleUnlimited and now available in audio! Check out the reading order below:

Stay with Me
Even when I'm Gone
Now Open Your Eyes

TALES OF WEEPING HOLLOW

For the reader who **adores centuries-old curses**, midnight tales, & magic. Inspired by classic horror novels, gothic romance, & the supernatural. Timeless, forbidden, & *haunting*. Available at most online retailers.

Hollow Heathens
Bone Island (coming soon!)

LINC & LO

A rockstar at rock bottom, a notorious party girl,
and a Chevy C10. What happens when two stars collide?

Enjoyed What If? Meet Ty's brother, Linc, in **Going Going Gone**, a rockstar romance set in California. Going Going Gone is a short story prequel and only available for free through nfgang.com. Check out the reading order below:

Going Going Gone: a rockstar prequel
City of Angels: a full length novel coming soon!

Find your next read at:
n f g a n g . c o m

ABOUT NICOLE FIORINA

Nicole is the author of the Stay with Me series and Amazon's #1 Best Selling Author in Gothic Romance for her debut in Urban Fantasy, Hollow Heathens. She lives in Florida with her husband, two kids, and lazy Great Dane, Winston.

Her writing style is *"insanely romantic"* and *"wildly addicting,"* striving to push hearts and limits. When She's not writing, she's either listening to crime podcasts, watching horror flicks with her kids, traveling, or planning her next book adventure—with one hand on her laptop and the other balancing a mocha latte.

I LOVE HEARING FROM YOU!
https://facebook.com/nicolefiorinabooks
https://instagram.com/authornicolefiorina
https://tiktok.com/@nicolefiorinabooks

Official Website, Newsletter, NF Shop, & More:
www.nicolefiorina.com

n i c o l e f i o r i n a

DA
DA